THE LITTLE MATCH GIRL

ONCE UPON A TIME, THERE WAS A LITTLE ORPHAN GIRL WHO WAS VERY POOR.

SHE WAS HUNGRY AND FELT COLD, SO SHE WENT OUT TO SELL MATCHBOXES, AS SHE NEEDED MONEY TO BUY FOOD AND WARMER CLOTHES.

IT WAS CHRISTMAS EVE AND IT WAS SNOWING HEAVILY. PEOPLE WERE WALKING QUICKLY FROM SIDE TO SIDE, BUYING PRESENTS.

NO ONE PAID ATTENTION TO THE GIRL, WHO HADN'T MANAGED TO SELL A SINGLE MATCHBOX.

WHILE WALKING THROUGH THE SNOW-COVERED STREETS, THE LITTLE GIRL, WHO WAS VERY WEAK, DIDN'T NOTICE THAT A CARRIAGE WAS APPROACHING AND ALMOST GOT RUN OVER.

WHEN SHE JUMPED TO ESCAPE,
SHE FELL TO THE GROUND.

THE LITTLE GIRL GOT UP AND CONTINUED TRYING TO SELL THE MATCHES. AS SHE WALKED, SHE PASSED BY A HOUSE WHERE PEOPLE WERE WARM, HAD A PLENTIFUL TABLE, AND WERE CELEBRATING CHRISTMAS.

WHEN SHE SAW THAT SCENE, SHE FELT HER STOMACH ACHE FROM HUNGER AND CRIED IN SADNESS.

NIGHT CAME AND THE SNOW BECAME MORE INTENSE. THE LITTLE GIRL, WHO WAS SHIVERING FROM THE COLD, TRIED TO TAKE SHELTER AGAINST A WALL, AS SHE DIDN'T HAVE ENOUGH CLOTHES TO KEEP WARM.

SO, SHE HAD THE IDEA TO LIGHT A MATCH
TO TRY TO FEEL WARMER.

WHEN SHE LIT THE FIRST MATCH, THE GIRL SAW THE IMAGE OF HER GRANDMOTHER, WHO HAD PASSED AWAY NOT LONG AGO AND WHOM SHE MISSED VERY MUCH. WHEN THE MATCH WENT OUT, HER GRANDMOTHER DISAPPEARED.

SHE LIT ANOTHER MATCH, AND AGAIN, HER GRANDMOTHER APPEARED. SO, SHE BEGAN TO LIGHT ALL THE MATCHES SO THAT THE IMAGE OF HER GRANDMOTHER WOULD STAY CLOSE BY AND SHE WOULD FEEL LESS SAD.

WHEN SHE LIT THE LAST MATCH IN THE BOX,
HER GRANDMOTHER REACHED OUT TO THE GIRL,
GAVE HER A HUG, AND LIFTED HER UP HIGH.

THEY FLEW TO THE SKY, WHERE THEY BECAME
TWO BEAUTIFUL AND SHINING LITTLE STARS. AT
THAT MOMENT, THE LITTLE GIRL STOPPED FEELING
HUNGRY AND COLD AND FELT AN IMMEDIATE SENSE
OF HAPPINESS.

THE NEXT DAY, THE LITTLE GIRL WAS FOUND LYING ON THE GROUND, SURROUNDED BY BURNT MATCHES. SHE HAD HER EYES CLOSED AND A SMILE ON HER FACE.

EVERYONE WHO PASSED BY THE STREET STARTED
TO CRY WHEN THEY SAW HER IN THAT SITUATION.
HOWEVER, THE TRUTH IS THAT WHEN SHE NEEDED IT
MOST, SHE WAS NEITHER NOTICED NOR HELPED BY
OTHER PEOPLE.

THE END.